A Children's Book
Inspired by
Leonardo da Vinci

Funny Machines for George the Sheep

Géraldine Elschner • Rémi Saillard

Prestel

Munich · London · New York

Just like every morning, in his grassy plain
George is feeling blue. He has serious worries,
because whenever it starts to rain
he begins to shrink.

This is a real
problem
for a fine-looking white sheep.

Whenever a storm **breaks out**, his legs become shorter, and he grows **small**, small, small, like a mouse.

But when
the sun comes out,
he quickly becomes big,
big,
big again.
Phew! And he forgets all
about his worries until the next
big rain.

But George's shepherd is **troubled.**
What can he do about
George's odd condition?
—Let's go see the **vet!** decides Leo one winter day.

But no matter what they try, nothing works. Finally Leo says **"That's enough—** we have to find a solution once and for all!"

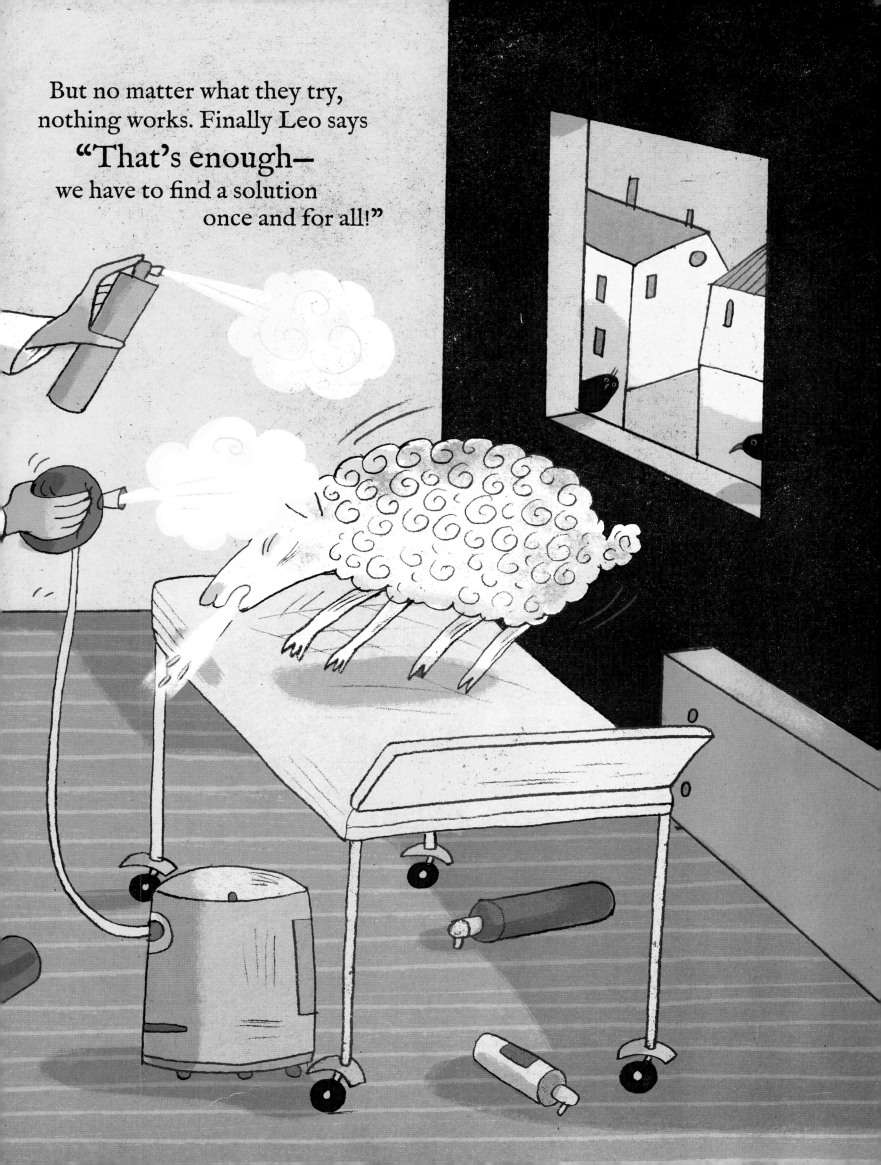

He goes into town, and buys a compass, some notebooks, **loads of paper,** a pointy triangle, some finely sharpened **pencils,** a circular protractor, a carpenter's meter, and last but not least, an **eraser** to erase everything and start again from scratch.

In a corner of **the pen**,
between the bed and the carpenter's bench,
he sets to work on his sketches ...

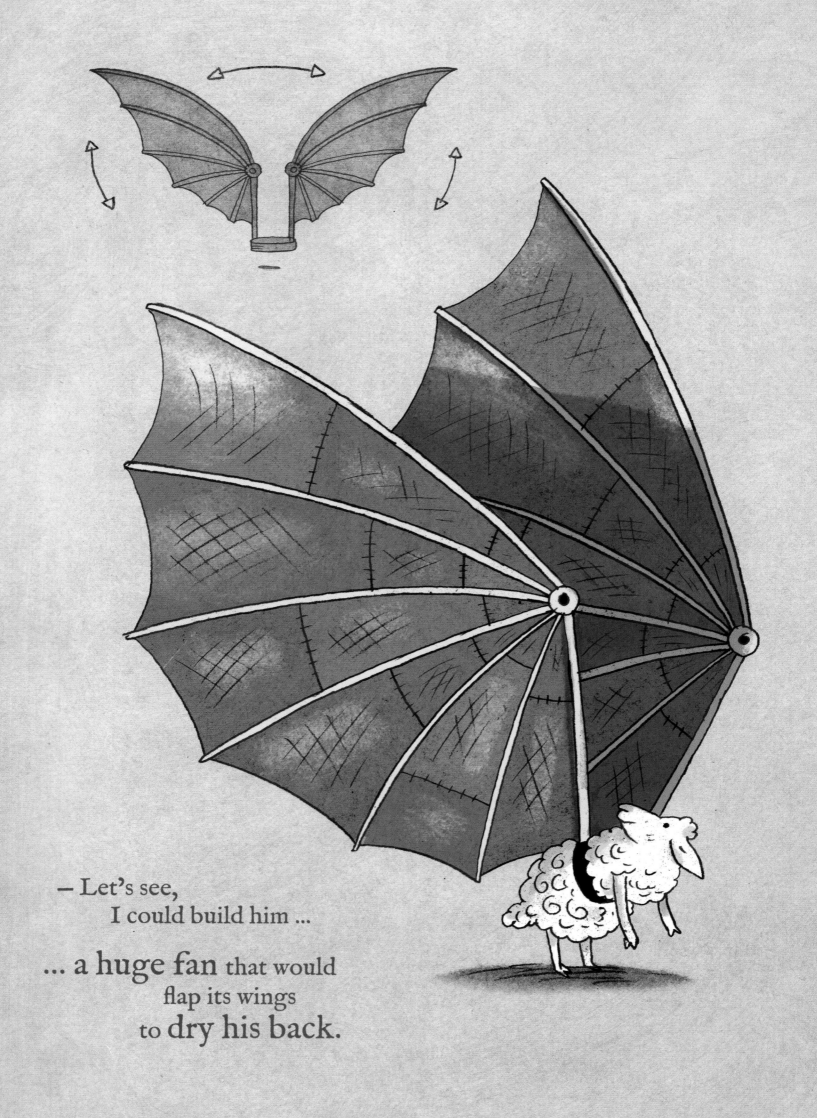

– Let's see,
I could build him ...

... a **huge fan** that would
flap its wings
to **dry his back.**

Or perhaps ...
... a small tank on wheels
that would be waterproof
against the smallest
drop of water?

Or what if I build him a a slightly lighter model,
more elegant, airier, and equipped with a sturdy floor?
The more he thinks about it, with his nose buried in his books,
the more sheets of paper he fills with secret symbols.

No one sees him for days.
Everyone is worried sick.
But finally, one bright new morning ...

Hooray!
George hops and
frolics excitedly.
His worries are gone.
Leo has built a **magnificent
shelter** just for him!

The shepherd smiles.
What a **beautiful umbrella!**
But at the first gust
of wind ...

whoosh

George takes off
from the field!

— **Come back!** cries Leo in vain
as his sheep disappears
into the distance.

In the fleecy sky, George soars through
the air, **filled with happiness**.
How pretty the earth looks from here!
He admires his grassy plain, his tiny friends,
and Leo's hat, which is now
no bigger than a bubble.

Then, between stratus, cumulus, and cirrus,
suddenly appears the most gorgeous sheep of all,
pretty and white as an angel!

His heart begins to pound,
dancing the samba and playing leapfrog.

Hop, skip, he comes a little closer and,
gently, trades **a little corner of his umbrella**
for a little corner of paradise.

—Wait for me, I'm coming! cries Leo
at the top of his lungs.
A shepherd, as everyone knows,
never abandons his sheep.

So he swiftly
gathers up his notes,
his compass,
his carpenter's meter,
and of course his eraser,
and begins to calculate
some more ...

With or without a machine,
he will find **his little George!**

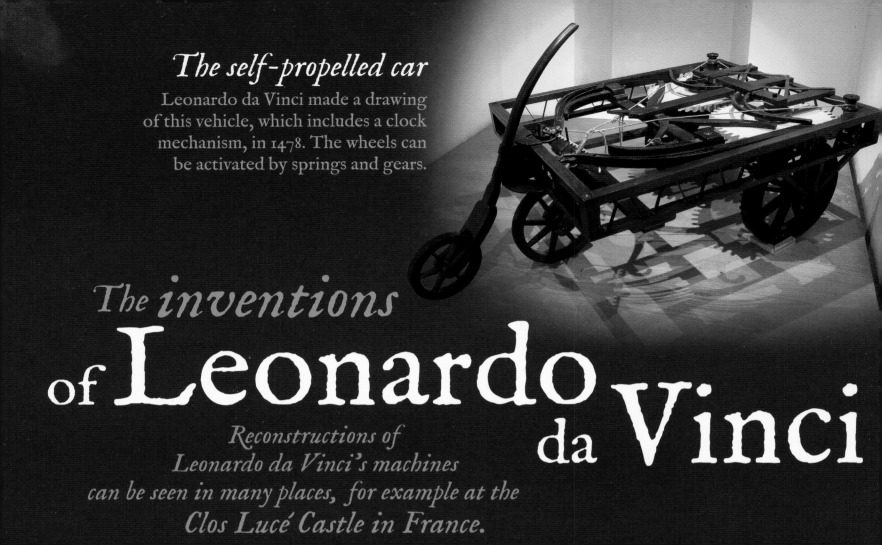

The self-propelled car

Leonardo da Vinci made a drawing of this vehicle, which includes a clock mechanism, in 1478. The wheels can be activated by springs and gears.

The inventions of Leonardo da Vinci

Reconstructions of Leonardo da Vinci's machines can be seen in many places, for example at the Clos Lucé Castle in France.

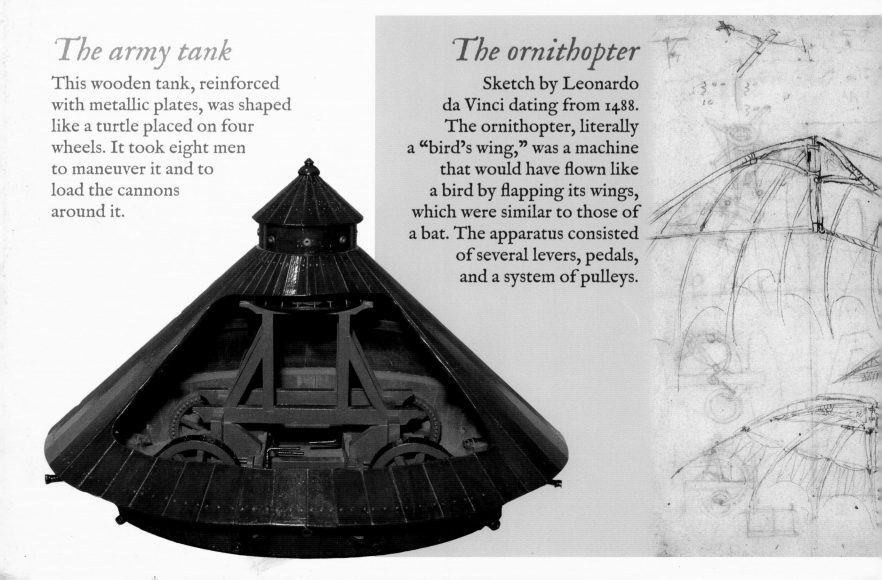

The army tank

This wooden tank, reinforced with metallic plates, was shaped like a turtle placed on four wheels. It took eight men to maneuver it and to load the cannons around it.

The ornithopter

Sketch by Leonardo da Vinci dating from 1488. The ornithopter, literally a "bird's wing," was a machine that would have flown like a bird by flapping its wings, which were similar to those of a bat. The apparatus consisted of several levers, pedals, and a system of pulleys.

The paddleboat

Paddlewheels turn in the water with the help of a steering wheel located on the boat. Even today paddleboats still use the same mechanism.

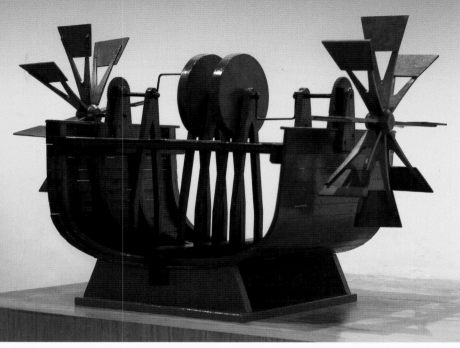

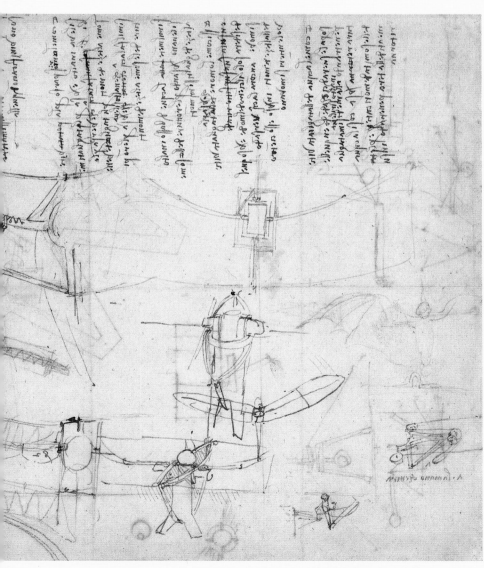

The parachute

Created between 1485 and 1502, this wood and cloth parachute is twenty-three feet wide and was tested in the year 2000.

Leonardo
da Vinci

1452-1519

Who was Leonardo da Vinci?

Leonardo was born on April 15, 1452 in Vinci, a village in Tuscany. Raised in the country, he loved nature and drew so well that when he turned seventeen he joined the workshop of the painter Verrocchio in Florence. He was a gifted and fast learner and soon painted better than his master. Throughout his life, Leonardo was invited to the courts of many great men. Today, the *Mona Lisa* remains the most famous painting in the world, and his village is now associated with this visionary genius of the Italian Renaissance.

In what way was he a genius?

Leonardo da Vinci was not only a painter, he was also a sculptor, a botanist, an anatomist, an inventor, an engineer, a scientist, and a philosopher—a universal mind, profoundly curious of the mysteries and workings of life. This genius who marveled about everything was also interested in mechanics and the military arts. As a result, he developed a series of unknown machines, imagined an ideal city, drew the human body with passion, experimented, and organized wonderful feasts. Nothing could stop this original and inventive man, constantly in search of new things to create.

What did he invent?

Leonardo's notebooks are covered with notes, calculations, and sketches that were all very advanced for his time. The list of his inventions is quite extensive: the first car, paddleboat, army tank, ball bearing, bridges, and machines. Inspired by the flight of bats, he even created flying machines. If none of these inventions saw the light of day during his lifetime, today's models reveal the accuracy and extent of his often unfinished works and their visionary nature.